The Portal

Samantha Gollakner

ISBN:978-0-578-59128-5

To all the people who have suffered in a battle they could not fight.

CHAPTER ONE: SENSITIVE

My Mom got pregnant with me when she was in her late-thirties. The doctor told her that she could not get pregnant anymore due to having had her right ovary removed when she was in her twenties.

She told him, "I am not getting an abortion. What is meant to be for this baby, is up to God to decide. Not for me to choose if it lives or dies."

Six months later, my Mom was enjoying a night in. Her body was wrapped in loose fit, black, elastic shorts and a red flannel, long sleeved shirt. The structure of her fair, bare feet were placed on the cherry red, wooden coffee table. Loose strands of her brunette hair, with red streaks was falling out of her attempt at putting the strands into a bun.

My Dad was running around the house trying to get everything together, so he could go bowling with some friends. His erratic figure was wearing a black, button down shirt, light shaded jeans with white, high-top sneakers. Strands of his long, dark brown hair bounced along the structure of his shoulders with every movement. His piercing blue eyes scanned the area of the room, ensuring that he had everything as he darted towards the front door while excitement flooded his form.

My Mother breathed in sharply, finding that something warm had fallen onto the surface of her upper lip.

She raised the shaken structure of her right hand towards her mouth to investigate further. She pushed her hand away allowing the pixels of her vision to burn red from the blood coming out of her nose.

His relaxed demeanor flooded his voice, "Honey, it is just a bloody nose. You will be okay."

Her tone flicked with an intense anger, "Paul. I need to go to the hospital, right now. Something is wrong with the baby."

My Father dropped the bag which held his bowling ball inside, to the floor.

He quickly aided my Mother into the car before rushing to Saint Peters Emergency room.

She was seen nearly instantly.

The doctor came into the room with a weary look on his facial image, "Your blood pressure was sky rocketing. That is why your nose started to bleed. We need to talk about the health concerns for both you and the baby, if you keep it."

Tears began to well inside of her glossy, blue eyes, "No. No one is taking this baby. I want to go home."

The doctor nodded once in understanding, "Okay, Teresa. We will get you sent home. Just hold on a little bit longer for me, okay?"

He left the room, but instead of going to get started on the paperwork, he went on the search for my Father. He finally found him in the waiting room, hoping for some answers fast.

The doctor's voice broke into the air of the ICU, "Gollakner."

My Father stood quickly, nearly stumbling over his feet, "Is everything okay?"

The doctor took a sharp breath, "No. I am going to have to be frank with you, Mr. Gollakner. The baby is already dead and if she does not abort the child, now you will lose your wife, too."

The structure of my Father's pupils expanded slightly, hearing this information, "Did you tell her this already? What did she say?"

The doctor lowered his gaze towards the glossy blue and white tile floor, "She said that the only one who is taking the baby is God, but if you give us the okay, we can take the baby. This is your wife and child. You can make the decision for both of them."

A single tear began to form along the right side of his vision, "Okay, I will do whatever you want. Just save my Wife. I already lost one of them, I cannot lose both."

The doctor nodded, extending his right hand over the empty space between them.

He rested his dominate palm on my Father's shoulder, "You are doing the right thing. I will have a nurse bring you out all the paperwork. We will get her into the operating room as soon as possible. Thank you for your cooperation."

My Dad hung his head down, his body filled with tension as he paced the area.

Finally, at 3:15 a.m. on March 27, 1996, a nurse appeared from the two, metal panel doors.

She approached my Dad with a gentle glow, "Gollakner?"

He nodded roughly, being unable to let any words escape in a calm manner, "Where is my Wife? Is she okay?"

She placed her open palms towards him in a relaxed gesture, "Yes. She is fine and so is your daughter. She was still alive when we did the c-section. Three months early, weighting in at one pound, fifteen ounces. She might not live through the night. If she does, it won't be for long. I am sorry. You can see both of them shortly, your wife is now in recovery. With the small possibility that your daughter will live. I have to tell you, she could have some defects."

CHAPTER TWO: THE MOVE

Six months later, we found ourselves moving to Minnesota. The railroad my Mom worked for was bought out by a bigger one. This forced all of the Dispatchers to move.

We did not stay there long. After the first major snow fall knocked the power out, I was only four pounds with a heart monitor.

My Mom became fearful of my life being jeopardized if we would have stayed in those conditions. So, that was when we decided to live somewhere warmer. After that moment, it was official, Texas became our new home.

At first, we were living inside of a small motel that the company placed us in while we could get settled in.

Not long after, My Dad met a man, who just happened to sell houses.

That day my Dad came home with great news to tell my Mother, "Teresa! Hey! I met a guy today, really great dude. Anyway, he sells houses. I told him we might be interested in one."

The small excitement that was on her face began to melt away, "Paul. We cannot afford a house, if you want to be a stay-at-home Dad. No, find something else."

My Father increased his voice with information, "Do not worry about that. He said they are a really cool house on wheels."

She twisted her eyebrows slightly, "What? Are you sure this is not some kind of a joke?"

A few days later, we found ourselves standing by a road, looking onto an empty, acre lot. It might not have looked like much at that moment, but once we were finished putting the house on the lot, it looked perfect.

It was not enough for my Dad though. He wanted it to be the nicest house on the block. He put on two, wooden decks, the one in the back was built around a three-foot-high, above ground pool. Both of the decks were stained red to match the shutters that seemed brighter due to the pale white that covered the rest of the structure. Connected to the left side of the house was a shed which my Dad also built with my Brother.

We parked alongside the home in front of the shed, on a gravel driveway that he laid. The walkway traveled through the yard to the road, weaving between a luscious sea of plant life.

When you walked into the wooden, white painted door, you were welcomed in by a burgundy shaded carpet with long strands that covered the living room. From there, you would have had some options. If you went to the left, you would be in the master bedroom and bathroom suite. If you were to go straight, you would find the kitchen, pantry and the backdoor. Then finally, go to the right and you would have found yourself in the dining room, den, guest bed, guest bathroom and of course, my room.

Moving in, we knew nothing about the land or the area. All we were given for information was that it was in the middle of nowhere in a small town, it had never belonged to anyone and we were very happy to hear that we were the only people to ever have lived in this house.

CHAPTER THREE: BOO-BOO

It did not take us long to settle into the new home. Everything was going great until I made a new friend.

I do not remember her much. Now as an adult, the only memories of her I have are the ones that other people, such as my parents would tell me throughout the years.

My Mother told me that my friend caused me nothing, but trouble in my life.

It would appear that ever since she arrived, I was an absolute nightmare, almost as if she was telling me to do harmful things. I was having horrible temper tantrums, constantly disobeying my parents. They did not think too much into it at first, just blew it off as me being in my terrible twos. Until I was a little older and the behavior had only gotten worse.

My new friend had followed us everywhere. She went to the grocery store, ate dinner with us and spent the night every day.

When I was around four years old, my Mother tried to release me from the restraints of my safety harshness from the car. She leaned forward to unlatch the main belt, when I bit her really hard on the right shoulder.

I do not remember this incident happening, nor do I know why I did it, but I do remember her yelling at me, "That hurt, Samantha. You know, ever since your friend has started coming around you have been very bad."

Hearing that word, *bad* always has made me feel horrible. I guess, not too long after that my friend went away.

My parents always thought that she was imaginary, like most little kids had, but mine was different.

She was a young girl in a misty, white night gown. She had shoulder length, brown hair and drops of honey for eyes which were more than real. She was covered in burns and wounds, I always called her Boo-boo. Due to my Mother calling my injuries, *boo-boos*. Her appearance in itself gave my parents reason to think that there was something not right with me.

CHAPTER FOUR:
NICE TO MEET YOU

When I was around five years old, I had an interesting experience that I will never forget.

One night, my Dad was tucking me into bed. Normally, I would watch the television until I would get so exhausted that I could no longer hold my eyes open, but that night was different. I remember slipping into a deep state of relaxation.

A few hours later, my Father said that he had heard me talking to someone. He immediately jumped up to go investigate. When he rounded the corner, getting a small glance into the room, the hair on the back of his neck stood straight up to a point.

The reflection in his pupils, portrayed me sitting in the bed, leaning over the railing to shake someone's hand.

My Dad's voice deepened, after not seeing anyone in the room with me, "Samantha, who are you talking to?"

Excitement poured from my lips, "Grandpa. He brought a dog with him! Oh and he says that he loves you very much."

My Father gulped in a harsh manner, "Go to bed, now."

He shut the door right after, not staying to see if I had followed orders.

His form walked towards the den as his mind rushed with memories of his deceased father. They hit him like a flashback, starting from when he was a boy until the day he died.

The last image that marked his vision was of his father's last moments, a harsh gasp was stolen from his lungs.

CHAPTER FIVE: SLEEP OVER

These types of experiences might have become normal to us, but we seemed to have forgotten that other people did not find it so calming.

Around my seventh birthday, my Mom's Mother came down to Texas for a visit.

We had a spare room and she decided that she wanted to stay in there.

The first night, I could hear her across the hall talking to herself. I could not make out the words, due to the walls that separated us. Next thing I knew, I was able to hear the echoing pound of her bare feet slamming into the carpet, going away from the room.

My heart began to rapidly beat against my chest as I pulled the covers over my head allowing my ears free range to listen out for any signs of what could have been going on.

My Mom's voice rushed into my mind, "Mom, just stay in the room. There is nothing in there. I am telling you, it is okay."

The sound of my Grandma defending herself in a shaken tone cracked through the wall, "Teresa, I am not staying in that room. If you think it is okay then you stay in there. I will sleep in your bed."

My Mother's shoulders slouched slightly, "Are you being serious?"

The weight of my Grandma's head fell forward in a fast manner, "Yes. What is the difference, Paul is already awake for the night. He is not going to be in there and I need to get some sleep. I am exhausted, but I do not want to sleep in there. It is scary. I keep hearing something chewing and scratching against the inside of the closet door."

A large breath of annoyance fell from my Mom's bottom lip, "It is probably just a mouse."

Her response was rapid, "Then you stay in there with the mouse. I am going to bed. If you get too scared, come sleep in bed with me. No one should be in that room, it is ridiculous."

The next morning, I awoke to the sound of a silent house. I crawled out of bed to go investigate to see who was up.

When I zoomed into the hall, my vision danced into the area next door which was supposed to be filled with my Mother's sleeping body, but it was empty.

My groggy form wondered through each room, not being bombarded by the sweet smell of coffee and cigarettes that usually lingered in the air above my head.

The house was dead silent, meaning my Mom must

have gotten spooked by the room as well the night
prior.

CHAPTER SIX: SLEEP STALKER

I was never afraid of that room, I didn't let the night my Grandma ran away scared frighten me, either.

Until one evening, nearly a year later. I went to bed around nine at night, like every other night that I had school the next day. I found myself waking up in a cold sweat, nearly gasping for air.

It did not take me long to ground myself. I began looking around the room, when I spotted the flashing lights of the time being shown on the VCR. It informed me that it was currently 3:15 a.m.

I tossed and turned before finally getting out of bed, being unable to fall back asleep.

I headed into the den, to find that my Dad was already up, tapping away at something on the computer.

The weight of my steps were so light, I was able to sneak up behind him, "Dad?"

His body jolted in response, "Yes?"

My vision dropped slightly, "Can I sleep out here on the futon?"

He nodded his head once, "As long as you sleep,

I do not care."

My figure darted for the black, cloth mattress, the metal frame creaked under my weight as I tried to settle in.

I closed my eyes gently, but sleep was the furthest thing from my mind. It felt like someone was staring at me.

I wanted to open my eyes to search the area, but at the same time, I was afraid of what I could possibly find lurking in the shadows.

Finally, I worked-up the courage to open my vision receptors. My frightened mind was far too confused to look away without more information. My vision started to adjust better to the lighting allowing me to make out the dark figure of what looked to be a half-human creature, but it was hard to decipher the details.

A rush of fear ran through my tiny form. I quickly threw the blanket over my head, the quivering was so bad, it looked as if my figure was being rocked.

I wanted to scream out and yell for my parents to come save me, but I had no idea how to explain to them what was going on. I did not even feel like I had enough strength to get the words to come out of my mouth during that time.

After that day, I remember always feeling afraid, but of what? I was not exactly sure.

All I knew was, something changed in me. The thought of there being something truly evil out there, just waiting in the darkness for its next victim would be enough to steal anyone's night sleep.

CHAPTER SEVEN:
THE PORTAL

The day was June 15, 2005. It started out amazing. It was so great, I wished every day could have been that nice.

I found myself slowly waking up to the morning sun kissing my face over the horizon.

It did not take me long to find my daytime legs under the weight of sleep pressing on my mind. I used the back of my right hand to remove the sleep from my eyes, walking into the den.

Surprise flooded my mind to see that my Dad was still sleeping, *'He must have taken a nap.'*

I approached the side of his current sleeping quarters to give him a slight shake, "Dad, hey. Wakey, wakey."

His blood shot, blue eyes broke open, they looked even brighter than normal against his tan skin, "What is it? What is wrong?"

My demeanor had shifted slightly under the question, "Nothing. I just wanted you to wake up."

He smiled gently, squishing his vision together tightly, "Okay, I am up."

The next thing I knew, the house was flooded with the smell of coffee.

The steam of the beverage fogged his thick, square rimmed, reading glasses that were held together by a metal frame, "So, what do you want to do today?"

I acted as though I was searching my mind for the perfect answer, but in reality, I already knew what I wanted to do, "Ride the four-wheeler!"

My excited form was drenched in an unpleasant tone draining from his mouth, "We have to fix it, remember? If that is the case then let's go."

I nodded my head firmly in understanding.

The sound of the plastic mug hitting against the countertop rang through the empty space, "Ready?"

The next few hours we found ourselves exhausted, covered in dirt and sweat but still, no answer as to why the motorized vehicle would not turn over.

He used the back of his right forearm to wipe the sweat running from his brow, "Time for lunch. I am starving."

I nodded gently in agreement, "Ravioli?"

He pushed his head forward in a silent motion of understanding.

We finished the food items within a matter of minutes. The rest of our day was spent playing around in the pool.

Our fun became disrupted as he rushed to the side of the pool. A small groan of discomfort was released from his lips.

My attention fell solely on him, everything else seemed to fade away, "Dad! Are you okay?"

My small lungs barely allowed my voice to reach him.

A moment of silence occupied the space, "Yes, I am fine. It is just heartburn. Give me a moment."

I sat patiently on the edge of the pool, waiting for the illness to leave his form.

My mind started drifting off towards all of the other times when he would become sick like this. Normally, a glass of milk or chalky tablets seemed to ease the discomfort.

The sound of water trashing caught my interest. It shattered my thoughts to see my Dad coming at me in a playful manner to throw me around the pool.

I screamed out in joy as I attempted to swim away from him.

He stopped the fun abruptly, looking down at his watch, "Hey, it is almost four. We have to get inside and make dinner. Your mom is going to wake up soon."

The amazing smell of baked chicken, mashed potatoes and corn filled every crease in the house as we made our plates.

After all of the food was gathered, we all flooded into the living room to watch television while we would enjoy the lavish taste of super.

Three bites of chicken in and my Father's face began to strain with agony.

He tried to clear his throat as if something had gone down wrong. He silently placed the plate on the black, wooden coffee table before he headed into the kitchen, hoping to find something to relieve it.

The sound of the seal on the fridge door broke into the air, informing us that he went to go get a drink of something cold, probably milk.

A loud thud trailed into the living room, coming from the kitchen.

My Mother rushed out of the recliner, putting her plate down on the table as well.

Her eyes met mine, "Your father."

When she rounded the corner, she screamed out, "Paul!"

I found myself standing in the entryway of where the kitchen and the living room connects. I could do nothing in that moment other than stare at his convulsing figure.

My Mom began to panic. She threw all of her weight to the floor, sliding on her knees.

She grabbed him by the shirt and started pulling him closer, "Paul. Do not leave me, damn it. You cannot leave me here. I need you. Please, Paul. Please."

Her eyes widen when they meet mine, "Go get the phone, now!"

I rushed into the living room, knocking the phone free from the dial. Once I got a hold of it in my clammy palms, I ran back into the kitchen.

My Mom called for a medic, they inform her that the nearest one was over a forty-five-minutes away.

She called my Brother next, "Jason. Hurry, I need you. Something is wrong with Paul. He is—"

My Dad had now completely stopped moving and a purple tint began to overtake his form.

She threw the phone across the floor and started to give him CPR.

Well, she had tried. Due to him going through that fit a couple minutes prior, made it impossible to give him proper breaths, due to is tongue being curled in his mouth. All she got to do is one breath in his mouth and three chest compressions.

I hate that I had no idea what exactly was happening.

I found myself standing on the right side of him, only a few inches separated us.

A nervous laugh slipped out of my throat, capturing my Mother's attention, "What the hell is the matter with you? This is not funny, he is dying!"

She stopped mid-way of the third compression, throwing all of her force from adrenaline onto me in the form of a shove, "Go look for the ambulance! Now! Go!"

She wanted me to get out of the room and not have to see what was happening.

My body stumbled into a backward step before tripping, throwing all of my weight into the cabinets.

I was unable to feel any form of pain in the moment. I could not convince my body to get up and follow her commands. All I could do was sit on the floor, blankly staring at my Father's lifeless form.

My Mom's last attempt to bring him back, does not fail.

All of the sudden, a long whistle of a wind pushed from his lungs and color began to erupt throughout his tan form.

His head popped up, looking at me then my Mother.

It took him no more than five seconds to jump to his feet and take off in a different direction.

My Mom began to pray in her head, *'Thank you, God. Thank you. Thank you. He is going to be okay.'*

His destination was the guest bathroom.

My Mom grabbed the back of his shirt, "Paul, you need to lay down, the paramedics are on their way."

He threw his head over his right shoulder slightly, "Let me go."

The moment he broke free from her hold, a neighbor walked in that my Mom had also called when my Dad was convulsing.

My Mom greeted the woman in a panicked tone, "He died, but he came back."

My Dad noticed her and leaned his weight on her shoulders, she started walking with him towards the bathroom. She looked to be around her late sixties. Stands of her messy, box colored, red hair fell around the tan complexion of her facial structure.

She started initiating a conversation with my Father as he sat on the closed toilet.

He looked towards her, knowing my Mother was standing in the doorway.

He leaned towards the woman, whispering something into her ear.

The neighbor turned towards my Mom, "Teresa, go get a cold towel, now."

My Mom rushed to get the piece of cloth.

I followed her movements as we ran back into the bathroom, "Okay, I got it."

She stopped sharply, staring at his lifeless form, "He is gone, isn't he?"

Her voice trembled, "Yes."

My Mom felt the strength of the emotions overpowering her, "You knew he was going to die, yet you sent me away. Why would you do that?"

Her voice grew deeper, "He said that he did not want you or Sam here. He told me to tell you, *I am sorry, but I can't do this anymore.*'"

I was taken out of the house by my Brother, who was twenty-six at that time.

It was easy to tell from the look on his face that he did not know how to help me. The only thing he did know was that he wanted to do something to make the pain I was feeling go away.

When I was out on the porch, waiting for someone to come get me. I started to look up towards the sky, seeing a golden cylinder of light coming down towards the house. It was shining through the roof, right where my Dad had last been seen by me in the house.

My left, index finger rose towards it, "Do you see that light?"

My Brother squinted his eyes gently, "No. What light?"

My eyes widened, *'This must be the portal to Heaven.'*

A few hours had passed since my whole world seemed to come crashing down on top of me. I was terrified of everything, but the thought of one day living a normal life was enough to get me through the tough nights.

A few hours later, I could not feel any emotion, not a thing. I ended up staying the night at my Brother's house the night my Father died.

Him and his wife placed me in the guest room on an air mattress.

I fell asleep almost immediately, desperately wishing that all of this was nothing more than a nightmare.

Four hours later, I woke up gasping for air. I could feel sweat running down my face.

My entire body shook, *I was standing in the den watching the paramedics work on my Dad before my Brother pulled me away. I could feel the energy in the room shift as a hazy figure of my Father rose from the body. His eyes meet mine with pain as he lowered his right hand down towards the body, "What happened today was bad, but I want you to know that where I am right now. I am okay."*

The blurred image of my mind trying to detect real from imagination caused my figure to run through the small hallway of my Brother's house.

It did not take me more than a few seconds to end up on the side of his bed.

In a frantic pant of a breath, I spoke softly, "Jason, can I sleep in here with you? I am scared."

He immediately jumped out of bed as if someone had placed an alarm against his bed side table.

His groggy vision fell over me, "Sam. What is it? What is wrong?"

My tone was weak in comparison to his, "I am afraid to sleep in there."

He rolled his head to the right, where his vision draped over his still sleeping wife, "Hey, babe."

Her words fell from her tongue in a discarded manner, "Yeah, what?"

He whispered softly, "Will you help me go get the

air mattress out of the other room and put it in here by the end of the bed, so Sam can stay in here?"

The weight of her torso lifted slightly, "Why can she not just sleep in there?"

His jaw tightened gently at her response, "She is scared of something. Come on."

I stood in a realm of guilt, watching them both maneuver themselves out of bed and into the other section of the house.

Before leaving the room, Jason turned to me, "Do not go anywhere. We will be right back."

I nodded in silence, not being entirely sure what was happening.

My figure shook violently under the sound of them sliding the bag of air against the hardwood floors.

The next thing I knew, we were all fast asleep, but I was afraid of what I might have seen when I closed my eyes.

It took me a longer time frame than usual before I drifted off into another world, a world where my life was still normal.

CHAPTER EIGHT:
CURSED STREET

It had been two months since the death of my Father. My Mother had to go back to work three weeks after his untimely passing from one world to the next.

She had called my Aunt and Grandmother to come down to Texas from Wisconsin to stay for a while to assist her in dealing with me, since my Dad was normally the one to take care of me while she was at work.

It was an early morning in August, the second day of the month.

The landline began to ring off of the dial.

My Mother picked it up in a flash, not allowing it to get past the second attempt.

Her right hand covered the structure of her mouth as a stream of tears ran down her face.

She did not say a word, not even a goodbye as she clicked the oval, end button on the plastic casing of the land line.

Her shaken, right hand placed it back onto the receiver.

My Grandma stepped forward slightly, closing the space between them, "What is it? What is the matter?"

She looked as though she was going to faint, "It is Johnathan. He was in a car accident on the way to work. We do not know who hit him or what happened, but the person who did it, they did not stop. He was shot into incoming traffic, where he was hit a second time. It tore the passenger side of the car completely off before throwing him into a tree. The crash killed him on impact, his chest got crushed between the steering wheel and the back of the seat. They said that he died instantly."

My Grandma reached over to give her a small embrace, but my Mother pulled away, heading towards the front door without saying anything else to anyone.

My Grandma tilted her head to the right, "Teresa, where are you going?"

Her eyes flooded with pain, "I have to go claim the body. They want me there."

My Grandmother became defensive over her, "You are in no state to be driving, right now."

My Mother shook her head, "I am not, the neighbor is going to give me a ride. You stay here with Sam."

The fast flick of her blonde hair leaving the house, flooded my vision.

A few days later, we found ourselves in the same funeral home, in the same room, with the same people.

My Mother walked into the room and her face turned whiter than the flowers in the vase beside her. It looked as though she was going to faint.

Someone had to walk her down the aisle allowing her to see the body. After she got to say her goodbyes, she stood outside the rest of the time. It was just too much. We were there less than two months ago for my Dad. The wounds were just too fresh.

During the next six months, it seemed like everything we knew for the last nine years was crumbling around us. With my Dad and Johnathon both being gone, it seemed as if some kind of domino effect was occurring. We lost four more people in the neighborhood that were close to us like family. It seemed like everything we ever knew was being taken away, one by one.

Although, it was not just death that was torturing the neighborhood during this time. People were also being hit by financial trouble as well as illnesses.

Nearly eighty percent of the people around us were either not able to afford their bills or lost their home all together.

The neighbor to the right of me, was walking around in his front yard barefoot, when a spider bit him. I guess, he did not take it too seriously. It had gotten so bad, he had to have his toe amputated. The surgery caused him to lose his job and his property as well.

The people in the surrounding areas, began to hear of the troubles, leaving them and the kids to place their own theories about what was going on, their conclusion was that our street was cursed.

That reputation only got stronger as the days passed by. It became such a house of hell, even we started to question, *'Was this a curse?'*

CHAPTER NINE:
DARK DAYS,
DARKER NIGHTS

Life seemed to have a major grudge against me and my family. One night, me and my Mother were sitting in the living room, when the television began to turn itself on and off. We immediately shot our attention towards one another trying to find out the reason behind this strange phenomenon.

The glossy tint to our vision began to fade as the corner of our sight fell against the black, wooden coffee table. Atop, sat the remote.

A nervous laugh slipped out of her mouth, "That was weird. Maybe, the remote needs new batteries."

The weight of my head fell forward, "Yeah, you are probably right."

My right, open hand extended away from my form, less than halfway through the motion, we heard a click.

This made me freeze in midair above the table.

It was the television turning itself back on. This time, it shifted to a different channel as well, the Packer game.

I could see the stress melting away from her face, "Oh, thank goodness. It was just your father messing with us."

Silence was the only response she received as I attempted to resort my hazy mind, *'Maybe. Maybe, it is him. Yet, if it was, why do I feel so afraid? Wouldn't his presence give me peace, the way Grandpa's did?'*

My thoughts were shattered by the crack of her raspy tone, "Are you going to put it back to what we were watching?"

The weight of my head fell forward as if beyond my control, "Yes."

I pushed the rubber surface of the button labeled, *last* on the black remote.

I slowly sank my body back into the fluffy material of the couch, but relaxing was the furthest thing from my mind.

A few weeks later, I had bought a new pair of headphones. The kind that belonged to a phone or similar device allowing the pieces to fit directly into your ear.

I was so excited to use them the next day on the bus to school. I unwrapped them from the plastic container, it creaked through the empty air.

My hands shook as I placed them on the glass kitchen table, knowing that as I went along my morning routine, I would make sure not forget them.

The next morning, I was awoken with a cheerful glow about the positive day ahead.

My first thought was on the headphones, I rushed through the *getting ready* phase of the morning faster than normal.

I quickly left the bathroom, heading towards the dining room, where I was last night when I put them in the perfect place.

The weight of my body rounded the corner and my vision melted over the tangled pieces. I could feel the push of confusion rushing against my facial structure.

I walked with a faster stride, hoping to get an answer as to why they were broken.

I carried the messy, revealed wires to my Mom, "Look what happened."

She pushed the square, metal frame exterior of her vision, lowering it onto the structure of her nose as she peered up at me, "What did you do to them?"

My shoulders strained in a defensive manner, "I did not do anything! I swear!"

She shifted her attention back towards the false light of the computer screen, "Right. Okay, Sam. Who did it then? Tigger?"

Both of us simultaneously moved our eyes towards the full grown, collie-chow mix laying on his right side, staring back at us.

My mind shot through thoughts, *'It could not have been the dog. He never does stuff like this. Plus, he was sleeping in my room with me all night. There is no way this could have been him.'*

The trail of my mind was broken by my Mother, "Sam? Come on, go get ready for school. Enough playing around."

My shoulders dropped in a defeated manner, "But, I am serious. Something happened and it was not me or the dog."

The weight of her head tipped back slightly in annoyance, "Go. Get. Ready. Now."

I sighed briefly, feeling like I was going insane. I was left with no choice, but to start keeping my experiences a secret, until now.

Tigger was lying beside me on the floor as we watched television together.

Out of nowhere, I began to feel his entire existence shaking.

I immediately pushed all of the weight in my form against the structure of my knees as I tried to investigate.

It looked as if he was having some kind of a fit.

My shaken, right arm extended towards the top of his head as I attempted to calm his disrupted figure.

His light brown eyes tilted towards me as if begging for help. He tried to move his body, but it seemed like something or someone was holding him to the ground. The chaos ended like it started—fast.

A deep breath left my nose, seeing that he was going to be okay, but the calmness of the thought did not remain peaceful.

The cockatiel bird in the kitchen was signing, *you are my sunshine,* something that he only did when someone entered the room.

The blood flowing through my veins suddenly froze as I pulled myself to my feet, walking towards the kitchen with a quiet step.

I did not make it halfway to the area when the energy shifted.

The bird began to release a high-pitched squawk that only occurred when he felt threatened.

A jolt of fear caused me to run back into the living room trying to hide my figure behind the couch as if I truly once believed that would be enough to stop it. Whatever it was. I did not know much about it, other than that it hid while destroying our lives—what a coward.

I attempted to control my breathing, when the air became stolen from my lungs as I heard the crack of the cabinet doors opening and shutting around me as if me and this entity were playing a messed-up game of hide n' seek.

Suddenly, the presence in the house felt lighter.

I took a deep inhale, *'Thank you, God. Thank you.'*

The house remained quiet for a few days until I was alone. The squeal of the hinges on the doors rang through the space causing my body to physically ache from the fueling fear.

That night, my Mother came home from work around 3:30 p.m.

Just having someone else there brought me peace. Her energy was dark, almost as if she was in internal misery.

My vision slid to the right as I watched her slip into an exhausted placement along the surface of the recliner. Seeing her in this form made my anxiety peak from fear, due to past events.

I stuttered slightly, "I do not want anything to happen to you."

Her head was in a leaned back position, "What are you talking about?"

I gulped loudly to the irritation lining her tone, "I

do not want you to die."

A loud puff of frustration began to linger in the air, "I am not dying!"

My opinion remained firm, "You do not know that!"

Her body leaned forward slightly as she yelled out in a rage, "Go away right now! Go do something— anything! Just get out of my face right now!"

I saw something zoom past my vision from the left. It landed directly in the center of me and her on the floor.

I stepped back slightly, my eyes widened in shock, "Did you just see that?"

See nodded, "See, that was your father. He threw that metal leaf off the wall to make you stop being so bad. Quit telling me I am going to die."

I tried swallowing, hoping to calm my dry throat, but I find nothing left to quench my thirst.

So, I remained silent, staring down at the object, '*I thought that I read the other day that spirits cannot throw things or hurt other people. This leaf was thrown at least a good three feet from the wall. It could not have just fallen like that, something had to have thrown it. I got this feeling that this is not my Dad we are dealing with. This is different, this is something else.*'

CHAPTER TEN: OUIJA BOARD

With me being older, it became more and more frustrating to be living that way, without any real idea of what was going on around me.

It was a Saturday, in the summer month of July. All of my friends were gone, except a few neighbors that I did not associate with. This left me with no one for company, other than the unknown entities that were lurking in the shadows.

I picked up my phone from the black, wooden coffee table. The weight of the Blackberry caused an indention to form on my left palm. Sadness dripped over me, seeing that I had zero missed calls or text messages.

The weight of my vision danced against the browser icon in my list of applications.

An idea shot through my mind as I typed something into the search bar, *'How to contact the dead?'*

My eyes exploded in awe as the first thing that popped up was talking about Ouija boards. I began to do as much research as possible, wanting to know exactly what I was getting myself into.

After barely denting five articles, I heard a soft, creaking echo through the silent house as if someone were walking along the floor of the kitchen.

That happening, only captivated me more to find out the truth.

I threw the phone down next to me on the couch as I ran into the spare room to gather the details needed to speak to the other side.

It said in the articles that you can either go to the store and buy one or make one from cardboard. With me being a broke teenager, I only had one option to pick from.

I quickly gathered two pieces of broken box and a black marker.

The structure of my legs carried me swiftly into the living room, where I began to build the speaking device.

Roughly an hour had passed. With the portal now completed, I found myself sitting on the burgundy carpet with my legs crossed on the floor, in front of the message board.

I inhaled a deep breath, closing my eyes as I asked my first question, "Dear spirits, can any of you hear me? If you can, please give me a sign."

No more than a second passed before the piece shot towards the *Yes* marking.

Seeing this, boosted my confidence in getting

answers. Finally, after all of this time, I am actually going to be able to see this clearly.

I wasted no time with pushing the conversation towards the direction I want it to go, "Who are you?"

I watched as it spelt out a male's name, *'P-A-U-L'*

A puff of air was sharply inhaled against the back of my throat, *'Dad?'*

My shaken hands trembled as the next question rolled out of my mouth, "How did you die?"

I could feel my patience beginning to run short as I waited for the reply, *'H-E-A-R-T-A-T-T-A-C-K'*

My mind reeled with excitement, *'Oh my, God. It is really him.'*

The board piece moved slowly towards the *Yes* symbol.

My eyes jolted in their sockets, *'Can he read my mind?'*

The cut-out object slid slightly away then straight back again, *Yes.*

I found myself now more captivated. I was more interested in trying to control my thoughts than focusing on the board.

The next thing I knew, the feeling of lightness had

left the room, leaving me once again to be alone.

My mind floored, *'I think I found a phone call to Heaven. This is the best day ever! I have to find out more.'*

A few weeks later, I found myself bored out of my mind, being seated with the neighbor watching television. His figure was placed next to me, leaving one cushion to stand between us as we watched the flickering images mindlessly.

My voice cracked the silence, "Do you need me to get you anything? Soda? Water? Food?"

His reply was faster than I assumed it would have been, "Just wish we had something to do right now."

I tried to hide my excitement, yet I could feel it tainting my words, "Do you want to play with a Ouija board?"

His head snapped in my direction, "What is that?"

I shifted my weight to face him, "It is a device that allows us to talk to the dead."

He ran his right hand through the short strands of his light, brown hair, "How do we use it?"

I pulled myself into a full stance, "Come on, I will show you. Before we can play, there is something you need to know. You cannot use this with just yourself. If you let go before the conversation has ended, the spirits can roam free. They are supposed to be trapped inside of the board, just waiting for someone to play with it in an attempt to get free. They can disguise themselves as something less intimidating, to gain your trust. Oh, and whatever you do, never ever burn the board."

Now, that I have explained the rules, we found ourselves seated on the ground, across from one another with the board laying between us.

His green eyes were filled with curiosity as I started the conversation, "Is any spirit here, that is willing to speak to us?"

The cardboard scraped against the main part before coming to a stop over, *Yes*.

He found his voice before me, asking another question, "Are you Sam's dad?"

My energy rose with hope as the piece moved to, *No*.

The smile on my face melted quickly, "Then who are you?"

It did not take long for the response to come through, '*A-B-B-Y*'

My attention shot up towards my friend, "I do not know anyone named Abby. Do you?"

He allowed his head shake to be the only silent means of communication.

I found falsified strength behind the next question, "What do you want? Why are you in my house?"

My eyes stayed glued to the board, '*T-O-K-I-L-L-Y-O-U*'

The fearful tracks in my mind raced through my thoughts, *'Kill me? Why do you want to kill me?'*

A few moments passed, '*Y-E-S-I-W-A-S-S-E-N-T-T-O-K-I-L-L-Y-O-U*'

My hands pulled back, releasing their grip in an automatic, fear-fueled reaction.

The neighbor's mouth dropped open, "Sam! I thought you said we were not supposed to let go of the piece until the conversation is ended properly! Then you go and break the connection? What is going to happen to us now?"

I raised both of my hands in a calming manner, "It is going to be okay. I am going to go have a cigarette. Do you want to come with me?"

He shook his head firmly, "I think I will just stay here."

My shoulders shrugged slightly as I walked out onto the front porch, where we found ourselves when we needed a nicotine fix.

While I was out there, I found myself pacing as if

something was looking for me and I had to try and find a way out.

My eyes glanced against something on the panel of the house, beside the front door. It was written in an ashy residue, *Abby*.

My bottom lip fell open as my right palm grasped the door handle, "Hey, come out here. You have got to see this. Hurry."

It took him much longer than I hoped for him to finally get out of the house.

I indicated with my shaken, right, index finger to where I wanted him to focus all of his attention.

After examining the weird writing, his bottom lip draped down, "Did you do this? Come on, Sam. This is not funny, anymore. I know you were the one who was moving the piece on the board then you came out here alone after being out here for a good amount of time while you were what? Marking up the wall? This is not funny anymore, okay? You won, just stop it."

I shook my head roughly trying to sort out my thoughts and his words, "No! Of course not. Why would I do something like that?"

I could hear the fear along his tone, "I think I had enough today. All of the sudden, I got really tired. I will see you tomorrow though, okay?"

He might have been tired, but I was frightened. I

wanted to go play with the board some more, but my anxiety pushed me not to.

When my Mom came home, I told her what we had been doing.

She became extremely angry, "What is the matter with you? Why would you do that? You know that those things are nothing but a bad game. Never play that again in the house. Do you understand me?"

My voice shook, "But Mom, it is a way for me to talk to Dad. He came through on the board."

Her head dropped slightly in disappointment, "Something tells me that your father, would not come talk to you through a cardboard box. Now, I have had enough of this conversation. It is over. No more."

She took the board outside to throw it away.

Hearing her words made a wave of relief wash over me, knowing that it is now gone or was it?

CHAPTER ELEVEN:
SHADOW FIGURES

Life began to slowly turn back to normal. Well as normal as we could be. Yet, I found my mind constantly trailing back to the board. Part of me wanted to make another one, to get more information about my Dad and now, Abby.

Thankfully for me, the other half of my mind stood firmly against the idea, *'Do not mess with those. You know they cause nothing but trouble. You were extremely lucky that nothing attached to you or that you were not possessed when you used it alone last time. No, no more.'*

The vibrations of my tangled mind carried me out of the house, leaving through the back door to get some air. I found myself turning towards out door therapy to try and ease the engulfed negative hold on my brain.

Finally, it felt like I was able to breathe once again. Something blew in the wind's currents, towards me from the east.

The weight of my jaw released upon visual of the object, *'Holy shit. It is the board, it came back.'*

I gulped roughly, running into the house. I could feel my entire form nearly paralyzed with discontentment.

Suddenly, I could tell my figure was beginning to calm down. My weight was then seated on the couch while I attempted to adjust my mind.

When another voice appeared inside of my thoughts, "Hello."

The structure of my eyes widened, '*What is going on?*'

I was unable to stick around for a reply of the unknown man, but I wrote down a note while running into the spare room, towards something I had saw earlier rush past my vision. It was hard to make out any definable detail. I saw nothing more than a black blur.

After searching the entire house, finding nothing, I felt more afraid than ever. I could feel the intensity of my body shake from inner anxiety crawling through my veins. The blood shot stains running along the whites of my eyes, grew more tired by the second.

I had not slept well since I was a kid, something about being in the dark, made me fear the hidden creatures in the shadows.

With day light piercing through the open blinds and nothing on the television to distract my mind, I tried my hardest to keep my vision perky.

Eventually, the tiredness of my soul won the battle, I drifted off into a deep sleep.

Yet, the sleep was never actually like what most people feel. I began to put myself into a lucid dream-like state.

The same dream I have had since I was a child.

I was standing at the base of a castle, built from beautiful, hand-crafted marble stone for the outer layer. It looked from the outside to be at least three story high.

I never got to go into the castle. The rustling of rocks shifting behind me, stole my breath from the chamber of my lungs.

I quickly turned around to be greeted by a large, brown bear. He snapped his jaws before lunging in my direction.

I took off running towards the castle, my mind fixated on the circular, stone staircase that wrapped around the building on the right side, leading towards the rooftop.

I could feel the cool sweat rushing against my face as I push my body harder with every stride. Yet, the stairs seemed to go on forever with no end.

Suddenly, I turned my head against my better judgement trying to determine how close he was to me. When I felt the locking hold of his jaws clasp around the bottom of my calf.

The scene would turn, to my bed room. Almost as if I was able to see through my closed lids, where I'd witness hundreds of gray, ashy wolves jumping through my window.

I inhaled sharply, hearing an unknown man's voice call out to me in a faded scream, "Samantha!"

My eyes shot open, looking around in a frantic manner attempting to verify with myself that I am in fact safe.

I just was beginning to relax, when a sharp, burning pain started to radiate from different areas of my body.

My attention was pulled first towards my right forearm, where the slashes of three nails lined my flesh. Seeing this caused the anxiety inside of me to boil. I felt myself slipping into a realm of panic.

The main focus of my interest shifted to a different area, the lower, left side of my stomach.

With me now being in a seated placement, I lifted the base of my black, t-shirt slowly. It revealed that the colors of a bluish, purple oval shape came into view.

I could feel the paranoia running through the fields of my mind.

I quickly tried to counter-act the thoughts as I mumbled under my breath, "It will be okay. Everything is okay. You probably were just harming yourself in your sleep by accident. This has happened before, remember? You will be okay. Just try and relax."

The self-motivation appeared to help me relax momentarily, until the intense burning on my left calf became too much for me to ignore.

I was reluctant to look as I pulled my injured leg

towards my chest to investigate further. My eyes widened sharply, seeing that in my flesh, was the after effect of a bite.

My heart began to pound rapidly against my chest, "What the hell happened to me?"

With this new information now riding through my mind, I began to feel helpless and afraid.

It took me less than two seconds to throw my body into a standing structure, taking off towards the front door.

I found comfort in being outside the house on the patio, where I decided to sit and wait for my Mother to return home from work.

Normally, she would get to the house around 3:30 p.m. I clicked the lock button on my smart phone, finding that the current time was only thirty minutes past noon.

I sighed briefly as my mind began to wander, *'What am I going to do for the next few hours? I cannot go back into the house, not without someone else here. I am too afraid of what might happen to me if I did go back.'*

It did not take me long to find something to entertain myself.

I allowed my mind to dance freely as I started to search the internet, looking for answers as to why this was happening and what it was that I could have done to fix it or if nothing else, just to understand the entities better.

I was able to find out some information such as mediums, the powers of old folk tale's ways to remove the spirits from the home. Putting holy water around every window and door frame warns away evil.

The more I read, I started to feel better about the situation, knowing now a little more about what was really going on.

My mind drifted away from the information and onto the light gray colored jeep that was pulling into the driveway. A rush of relief washed over me, seeing that my Mom was finally there.

She approached me with a gentle tone, "Hey. What are you doing outside?"

I shrugged my shoulder's slightly, not wanting her to see the fear flooding my form, "I just wanted to be out here, I guess."

I could tell by the look on her face that she did not believe me, but I did not want to bring it up and make her have a bad end to her day. So, once again I decided to keep it to myself, but this time seemed harder than the rest.

Her vision swept over my emotional figure, "You are not still afraid of the house, are you?"

Before I was given a chance to reply, she spoke in

a fearful tone, "What happened to your arm?"

My mind started to run on autopilot, "Oh, ha. Right. That. I went over to the neighbor's house to play with her cat, it must have scratched me."

The look on her face informed me that she did not know whether or not I was telling the truth.

She agreed to the explanation by changing the direction of the conversation, "Well, next time be more careful. Now, come on inside, we are going to make super."

I exhaled loudly. Finally, feeling at peace once again. For now, anyway.

When we walked into the dwelling, we found that something mysterious was going on.

Hundreds and hundreds of flies took over every inch of the house.

My Mother turned towards me slightly, "Did you leave the back door open?"

I shook my head firmly, "No, I swear."

Fear radiated through the vocal cords of her throat, "There are so many flies in here. What the hell is happening?"

Before I had a chance to answer, another stream of thoughts left her lips, "Hurry, help me kill them."

I nodded once as we both grabbed an old newspaper from off of the microwave, hitting the entire swarm of flies, ensuring that they were not going to come back. At that point, I had no idea what was going on.

My Mother turned towards me, "I will call your brother tomorrow to see what he thinks."

The next morning, we woke up to again more flies.

While we were walking around the house killing each one, my Mother was on the phone with my Brother, "What do we do? We have no idea where they are coming from, help us."

I could hear the faint echo of his voice, "Maybe, they are coming up from the drains. Try blocking them at night and see if it makes a difference."

She nodded slightly before hanging up the phone. That night, once all the flies were killed, we decided to give it a try.

Sure, as hell, the next morning we woke up to hundreds of flies.

My Mom's shaken form turned towards me, "This is all of your fault. If you would not be playing with that stupid Ouija board, none of this would have happened. Flies are a sign of evil."

CHAPTER TWELVE:
PARTY FOUL

It was a Saturday night in October, we had some people over for dinner and drinks. The drink of the night became vodka and lemonade. Roughly three drinks in, the sound of something falling in the other room caught everyone's attention.

It changed the conversation as everyone froze as they looked to my Mom for an answer to alleviate the silence.

A small chuckle escaped her slightly parted lips, "Do not worry, stuff like that happens all the time."

A neighbor named Jennifer, shifted her weight between the structure of her hips, "What are you trying to say, that the house is haunted?"

At that point, the rest of the company began to file out the front door to head home. I remember watching them leave, being engulfed by fear from the house.

My mind ran off track, *'It is not that bad, guys. I wish you were staying longer.'*

Now, there are only four people left. My Mom, Jennifer, Marcus and myself. My Mother shifted her eyes between the girl with light brown hair, staring down at her drink before allowing her focus onto the tall, lanky man beside her with short, dirty blond hair.

My Mom's voice cracked, "Yes, the house is haunted."

Marcus threw his head back laughing, nearly knocking himself off of the chair, "There is no such thing as ghosts. You guys are crazy."

With the shot of an insult being fired, my Mom's voice grew firm, "I am not joking with you. There is something wrong with this house."

Through a fit of laughter, he raised his hands in a playful manner, "Okay, okay. You know what, I will prove to you that nothing is in this house."

The weight of his figure slid off of the bar stool. Indentations of his form are still pressed down against the black, leather cushion. He walked to the living room, where we previously heard the noise coming from.

His voice bit at the air in a snarling grow, "Hey, spirits. If you are real then prove it."

His words began to taper off at the end as if he almost regretted saying anything at all. We found ourselves sitting in a realm of silence, waiting for something to happen.

When a few moments passed with nothing,

Marcus's confidence grew stronger, "Hello? Show yourself. Bite me, scratch me, shove me. Come on, make something happen to me. Oh, wait you can't do that because you are a coward."

The air in the house began to flood with the smell of sweat leaking from his pores. Again, nothing happened.

Marcus turned around to walk back to the chair, "See, nothing happened. You guys are just scared of nothing."

He looked down at his drink, his eyes were lined with fear, "Hey. How strong did you make these drinks, Jennifer?"

She pushed her lips into a downward, thinking manner, "I did not make them strong at all. Why do you ask?"

He turned his head towards her, revealing that his skin is leaking cold stream of sweat.

It ran down his pale completion, "I do not feel good."

My Mother stepped into the conversation, speaking in a comforting manner, "Go lay down on the couch for a while. I will make you some coffee to help you sober up."

He did not say a word, getting out of the bar stool, he headed straight for the couch. He practically threw his body onto the green shade of cushions. His form was positioned in a face down image as the sickness in his veins depleted all of his energy.

The smell of freshly brewed coffee rushed throughout the air currents. My Mother brought him a drink, but he did not respond to it.

Jennifer was wrapped in concern, her voice shook, "Maybe, I should just take him home. He does not look good at all."

She walked over to the couch, pulling on his right arm, transferring it up and over her head allowing it to lace around her neck as she began leading him towards the entrance.

She spoke in a breathless sway, "I am sorry that we have to leave like this. Thank you so much for having us over."

We watched them exit, stepping over the threshold.

All of the sudden, Marcus began to show life once again. It was almost as though the minute he got out of the house, he was fine. The sweating came to a halt, his face then held a brighter hue and he was able to stand on the structure of his feet without swaying like before.

Jennifer turned towards my Mom, "This is really weird, Teresa."

My Mom nodded her head slowly trying to wrap

her mind around what had just happened. They continued walking down the steps towards their vehicle.

My Mother slowly closed the door.

Before she was able to say a word, I took over the conversation, "So, whatever is in our house is what made him sick? Do you think that it could do the same thing to us?"

She released a breath of anxiety, "You are thinking the same thing as me, right now."

I swallowed sharply, "I am afraid."

Her head dropped in a forward manner, "Me too, me too."

CHAPTER THIRTEEN:
A FATHER'S LOVE

When I was younger, I had a best friend named, Nathan. We had met in high school and bonded over the fact that we were both gay.

One day, we were sitting next to each other in silence, when he spoke in a shaky tone of uncertainty, "Marry me."

I could not help but to release a harsh laugh, "Very funny."

His stare did not waiver from the ground.

He spoke in an emotionless whisper, "I am being serious."

I exhaled deeply, "So, what? Are you trying to tell me that you are really not gay and you lied to me just to get close to me?"

A slight smirk ran against the right side of his mouth, "No. I never lied to you and I am gay. It is just—it is complicated."

I tried to lighten the mood by speaking in an

upbeat tone, "Well as the woman you asked to marry, I deserve to know why that is even a question."

He shook his head firmly, "If I told you the truth, you would hate me."

I used my left hand to scratch the anxiety away that was crawling underneath my flesh, "Tell me now."

He inhaled sharply, speaking in a soft tone, "Okay. So, when I told my Dad I was gay, he did not take it well. He told me that he would not have a gay son and would kick me out of the house and disown me, if I did not find a girlfriend. During our fight, I just yelled out in the heat of the moment that you were my girlfriend, but now he wants to go with us to a movie on Friday, so he can get to know you and I can prove to him that we really are dating."

The structure of my shoulder's tightened, "Okay, fine. I will lie for you."

He wrapped his arms around my neck, "Thank you, thank you. I owe you, my life."

That Friday, I found myself sitting on the porch trying to figure out a way to get out of this before they got there.

Next thing I knew, a black sedan was pulling into the driveway.

I could hear the pebbles being shot in an upwards movement on the underbelly of the vehicle. It took everything in me, to walk towards that car. I slid into the backseat, finding that Nathan was already there.

The car ride to Denton was torture. The silence was so thick, I felt like I was going to puke. I nearly jumped out of the car when we arrived at the destination. Finally, getting some fresh air made me feel better. The movie went well, right after we headed back towards my house.

Nathan's Father told me to wait outside on the porch, telling me that Nathan would be outside shortly, they needed to have a father-son talk.

My anxiety had been off the charts all day, wishing I would have been firmer. I wish I would have just told Nathan no when this all began.

I saw the car door of the vehicle open on the passenger side as it illuminated the cabin from the overhead light. It was so dark, I was unable to see him approaching me. The sound of loose gravel beneath his shoes allowed me to determine his location. The vibrations of the wooden deck stairs creaked and moaned under his weight.

Now, that he became visible, he hung his head down low, "I need a weird favor."

My mind reeled with the possible outcomes, "What is it?"

He released a defeated sigh, "I need you to kiss me good night."

I was able to hold back a small fit of laughter, "No, I am not going to do that."

He began to walk towards me, he locked his clammy palms around my forearms, pulling me closer.

I spoke in a firm gesture, "Nathan. Stop it, now."

His tone cracked, "I am sorry, but my Dad said he would not believe you are my girlfriend unless we kissed."

I found myself still struggling to get away, his eyes glance above my right shoulder. His grip loosened as he took small steps backwards in fear, nearly falling down the stairs.

I tilted my head over the structure of my left shoulder trying to figure out what had frightened him so badly, but nothing was there.

My words hit him roughly, "What is the matter with you?"

His right, index finger extended towards the entrance of my house, "Your dad and brother are here."

I allowed my mind to process whether he was telling the truth, "Describe them."

He swallowed roughly, "Your dad is taller than me. He has short, dark brown, curly hair, bright blue eyes and a white t-shirt with the sleeves tore off. He has fraying, cut-off blue jean shorts, light wash in color. Your brother has short, red hair, his face is covered in freckles. He is wearing a light gray shirt, dark blue jeans and brown work boots."

A slight chill ran through my body, *'There is no way he could have known all that or what they looked like. We did not keep pictures out around the house of either one of them. He has to be telling me the truth.'*

He slowly took one step back, "I have to go now. Your dad is mad at me. I have to go now. I will talk to you later. I am so sorry for all of this."

I found myself watching him disappear into the darkness one last time. I remained in the same placement under the glow of their taillights until they had vanished.

A few hours later, I got a call from Nathan.

He was having a break down, crying on the other end, "Please, help me. Please, tell them to leave me alone. They followed me home. Please, I am so sorry. Just please, help me."

My facial image contoured with confusion, "Who?"

His tone cracked with fear, "Your dad and brother."

I spoke in an outwards motion, hanging up the

phone with Nathan, "Please, leave Nathan alone and come back home. I promise, I am safe."

After that day, I never spoke to Nathan again. The house terrified him that much. I understood though, if the tables were turned, I would have done the exact same thing.

CHAPTER FOURTEEN:
DEATH SENTENCE

When I was sixteen, I almost died. I dropped my weight down to the low eighties. I was so skinny and weak, my Mom had to carry me into the bathroom, so I could get clean because I always felt faint.

I was having heart burn so severely, it would turn my chest beet red and be warm to the touch. I went to doctor after doctor with them pushing me off onto the next. When they could not figure out what was wrong with me, they gave up. It was one of the worst things I had ever been through to date.

Finally, after not finding a reason to my illness, my GI specialist decided to do a scope of the inside of my body. I was terrified of what they were going to find. In the moment, I did not know what I feared more, them finding something or them not.

I woke up from the sleeping medicine to see that my doctor was standing beside me.

She spoke in a soft tone, "We found something. You have bleeding ulcers throughout your entire digestive system. There are blisters that run all through your body as well."

My Mom's eyes teared, feeling relieved that they actually found out what I was going through.

She spoke in a desperate tone, "What do we have

to do to cure it?"

The doctor's figure was engulfed with disappointment, "There is no cure. The way I see it, is you can give her some baby formula to buy some time. She is not going to last long."

My Mother was unable to take that as an answer. That night when we got home, we prayed to God to help and guide us down the right path.

Roughly three hours later, something in the house broke in the piping system. We had to call a local plumber to come out and give it a look, to see if he could fix it. He said that he could be out that way in the afternoon and that his wife was going to have to come with him, due to his van breaking down. It took them two hours to finally show up.

The wife was seated in the car, but my Mom felt guilty and invited her inside.

I was laying on the couch, too exhausted to even pick up my head.

The woman turned her focus onto me.

Speaking to my Mom with a slurred, drunken tone, "What is wrong with your kid?"

My Mother sighed deeply, "She has blisters all over inside of her body. She is slowly dying and nothing we try seems to be working."

The woman carelessly waved her hand towards my Mom, "No. She will be just fine. Get her some aloe juice. If she takes a few shot glasses of that a day, it will clear it up in no time."

My Mom tilted her head to the right in curiosity, "Aloe? Are you sure?"

The woman's confidence did not wavier, "If it can heal a burn on the outside, it can fix ones that on are the inside as well."

My Mother ran out that night to get me something that she finally thought would help me.

I started to take it that night then three to five times a day. Almost immediately, I was able to tell a big difference. Three months later, I felt like a completely difference person. I was actually able to eat, sleep and go back to school.

I was so happy to feel better, but in the back of my mind, I could not help but to wonder, *'Is the spirits in the house what made me so sick? Were they really trying to kill me? Is this Abby's way of proving to me that I cannot fight her?'*

CHAPTER FIFTEEN:

FORECLOSURE

Now, that I was finally out of school, graduating my senior year in nineteen days, the world seemed to have a whole new outlook for me.

Our finances were also hit hard, like everyone else in the surrounding areas.

We got tired of fighting with the entities we were unable to see.

My Mother decided to file bankruptcy, knowing that it was the fastest way of getting out of the house of hell. Once everything was filed, she had a month to get out of the house and find a new place to live. She did not know where she was going to go, but she wanted to be as far away from that house as possible.

I started to help with the packing, anything she did not use on a daily basis, went into a box.

A few days later, she started to have severe chest discomfort.

I had taken her to the emergency room, where they ran almost every test on her. All of them came out clean as far as the medical field was concerned. They told us that nothing was wrong with her, that she was just having panic attacks related to stress.

I was able to take her back home that night. Two days later, she started to show the same symptoms, chest pain that moved into her jaw and back. She began to sweat profusely through her t-shirt. She told me that she was in intense agony and that she had to go lay down for a while.

She started to tell me that she was becoming scared because at night she could hear someone calling out to her, a male's voice, "Hey."

She informed me that she handled it by turning over in the opposite direction from where she heard the voice, hoping that it would be enough to make them go away.

However, the voice only became more persistent, "Hey."

This only made her angrier, calling out, "What do you want? Can't you see that I am trying to sleep here?"

She said that the male voice was not heard from since, but the strangeness did not stop there. Later that night, she could hear a choir singing when she was trying to sleep, she said it sounded like angels.

With this information and her symptoms, I feared that she was on the verge of death, both of those were signs of it.

I did not waste any time to ask, "Do you need to go to the hospital?"

She spoke in a stranded tone, "No. I was just there. You heard them say that there was nothing wrong with my heart."

I could not allow her answer to sit right with me. I had already lost one parent, there was no way in hell I was not going to call nine-one-one.

I went outside to wait for the paramedics to get there. Finally, I was able to see that one of the transportation vehicles for the hospital was pulling into the driveway.

Two men got out, carrying in a bright red bag of supplies.

The older of the two's eyes lit up as they danced against my figure, "It was different with your dad, it will be okay."

I nodded my head once in understanding. I began to lead them through the house towards my Mother's room.

Within a matter of seconds, they were wheeling her to the portable hospital in the back of their van.

I watched in shaken distress, not sure how this was going to end. With tears sliding down both sides of my face, I fumbled with the key trying to place it into the lock.

Once I knew that the house was secured, I nearly jumped down the flight of stairs on the porch. My soles slipped against the gravel driveway. I knew I needed to relax, but my fear was too intense, I could not feel a thing.

I hurried into the vehicle, ready to chase the medics to the hospital.

My ears were muffled by the rapid pound of my heart, when a knock against the drivers side window snagged at my attention.

My shaken, left, index finger pushed down the button to roll the sheet of glass between us into the seal.

His posture was calm, along with his tone, "Promise me, you will not chase us. You could end up getting hurt and your mom does not need to have you injured, right now. I know that you are worried, but your mom is stable, she should be okay. It was different with your dad, he was already gone when we got here. She still has a chance. You saved her life today."

The amount of time it took to get to the Emergency room seemed like it was hours before I was able to see the hospital clearly from the top of a small hill underneath the asphalt.

I almost forgot to remove the keys from the ignition as I ran into the entrance that has emergency transports.

My frantic figure rushed over to a receptionist, "Where is Teresa Gollakner?"

I could tell by the look on her face, I was on her last nerve already and the conversation had just begun, "No, sorry. No Teresa is in the system."

I used the inside of my right hand to hit the counter, a shock of pain ran up my forearm, "She just came in here by the medics, I know she is here. Now, where is she?"

The lady began to understand why I was being so rude.

She picked up the black, landline on her desk.

I tried to listen into the conversation, hoping that I would be able to get some insight as to what was going on, but the words were too muffled.

Quickly, she reset the phone, without saying goodbye to the person on the other side, "Your mom is currently in emergency surgery. It is on the third floor."

A glimpse of hope shot through my body as I took off running towards the elevator.

My head tipped in the reversed direction, slightly yelling, "Thank you!"

I was able to hear the faded echo of her tone, "No running!"

Only, it made me speed up faster. Finally, I got onto the elevator.

Exiting the steel box, my feet pounded loudly as I entered the waiting room.

I was greeted with concern from a woman seated behind a desk, "How can I help you?"

My stress had me so wired I could hardly speak without my words being breathless and broken, "Where is Teresa Gollakner?"

She looked through a small window to the right which allowed her to see into another area that I could not, "She just got done with the surgery. The doctor just gave me the thumbs up, she is currently stable. You will be able to go see her in a minute."

I felt like my whole body was going to collapse, tears broke out of my eyes as I felt relief rushing through my form.

Somehow, I managed to drag my feet against the carpet, heading towards the uncomfortable, blue colored seats.

A nurse saw my distress, rushing over towards my right side, "It is going to be okay. She is going to be just fine."

In the moment, I wanted to pull my hand away from her embrace. The other half of me felt the need to break down and cry. Neither of which happened, all I could do is sit in a miserable silence as I stared at the dark blue colored carpeting under my feet.

Finally, I heard doors open in front of me, the image of my Mother being okay, relaxed me three times more than what I was before.

My shaken form followed the nurse, who was pushing the mobile bed towards the recovery unit of ICU.

The back of the nurse was the only thing I could see. Strands of his brown hair moved gently with every step.

The vocal expression of a woman alerted me from behind, "Excuse me, but you cannot be back here."

A flash of fear rose to my cheek bones as I came to a fast halt.

I began to stumble over the words, "Uh—my mom is right there. I just wanted to see her."

The woman's messy bun had loose strands of blonde highlights that shined against the dim lighting.

It matched perfectly with her pair of light pink scrubs, "I understand that, but I really need you to go wait in the recovery area. They are going to get her all-settled in. Once they do, I will come find you so you can see her."

My mind reeled, "Okay. Let's go."

Nearly an hour had passed and to my shock, I was finally called into the back room. I thought I was going to have to sit there forever.

My body shook, not knowing what to expect. I rounded the corner quickly, seeing that she was in fact okay. My heart felt like a ton of weight had been lifted from my chest. I wanted nothing more in that moment than to be able to ask her questions, but she was on the phone with her work, explaining to them the situation.

My head fell to the left, to see that my Brother was

standing with his arms locked against the structure of his chest cavity. His blue eyes remained held against her as his jaw tightened with the unknown future.

I leaned my weight closer to him, speaking in a soft whisper, "I think the house is haunted. I think whatever is in the house is what made Mom so sick."

His vision squinted sharply, "What?"

Before I had a chance to express my feelings, our Mother hung up the phone.

Her attention fell towards the nurse, "Can I go home now?"

The nurse could not help but to release a small fit of laughter, "No. You cannot go home, yet. You are far from going home. The doctor suggested that you have open heart surgery, more commonly known as triple by-pass."

My Mom threw her head back against the cushion, "Can I at least go outside to have a cigarette?"

CHAPTER SIXTEEN:

THE PRIEST

With my Mom being laid up in the hospital and with my Brother leaving to go on vacation to my Mother's orders. I was left to figure out how to move everything and pack alone.

It was not too bad during the day, it was at night when things began to come out of the shadows to prey on its next victim.

I decided to start on one side of the house, making my way through each room trying to ensure I did not miss anything.

With my brain being mainly focused on my Mom, it was very difficult to think of too much else.

The food pantry became my first target.

Everything was going smooth then all of the sudden, I hear a voice flowing through the air, "Samantha."

My entire form jumped in fear, my tone shook along with my figure, "Whose there?"

Again, the same unknown, male's tone flew through the air, "Samantha."

I walked around the corner, thinking that perhaps, I did not lock the front door and someone was just playing a joke on me. Nobody was there and all entrances were sealed, making my theory impossible.

My eyes darted towards the pink and orange rays of light that were just starting to break through the kitchen window. I sighed in frustration, knowing that something was going to happen soon.

I tried to get as much done as possible, but a creaking from the kitchen floor, informed me that I was in fact done for the night.

I rounded the corner, heading straight for the exit. The weight of shock flooding my bottom lip caused it to hang open, seeing that all of the cabinets were open.

My last inhale of air became stuck along the tunnel of my throat. I picked up speed, nearly sprinting against the carpet and out the front door. Once I was outside, my body collapsed into the fleshy wood of the entrance in relief.

My mouth began to ache from the fear that was building up along my jaw line.

I had to remind myself to breathe as if this entity had taken more than just my home, it started to overtake me as well.

It did not take me long to convince myself to walk towards the vehicle.

My shaken, right hand fumbled with the key as I tried firing up the engine, but all I was left with is the drainage of the new battery.

The state of my emotions were decreasing by the moment. The weight of my head fell forward, until my forehead slammed into the steering wheel, this was how I slept the entire night.

The sound of a diesel truck passing by on the road caused my mind to stir awake.

Through blurred vision, I was able to find the glowing, green clock on the dash that informed me it was four in the morning.

A loud sigh exited my chest as my eyes flinched in pain that radiated across the top of my back, from sleeping in such an odd position.

I placed the first cigarette of the day loosely between my lips.

The smoke rose in the car quickly, but I did not have the care to unroll the sheet of glass as I was still attempting to fully wake up.

A sudden wave of depression washed over me.

I could do nothing in that moment, other than feel completely helpless.

After sitting in the car for over two hours, a flash of light shined against my face, sparking an idea, '*What if the spirits are using the energy from my car to make themselves more powerful? They can do it to my phone and light bulbs, I have seen it. If they can do that, they can do anything.*'

I immediately put my idea to the test by rushing

out of the car, towards the rear end.

Knowing that the vehicle is in neutral, gave me a fair chance of pushing it towards the road. It started as soon as the front tires touched the gravel around the property line.

I wasted no time hopping into the drivers seat, taking off down the road towards town which was a good thirty-minute drive.

I pulled off of the main road and into the small parking lot of a Catholic church, I used to go to as a child.

My body remained unsure, with every step towards the door. It took me longer than I expected to enter the holy place.

I was immediately greeted by a woman, her dark brown hair bounced against her collar bone as she moved. The reflection of my exhausted form could be seen reflecting through her light brown eyes.

She spoke to me as if in confusion, "How can I help you?"

My gaze dropped towards her white shoes, "I need to talk to the priest."

Her posture shifted slightly under the question, "His is busy right now. You will have to come back another time."

I stepped forward, closing the space between us as I spoke in a strained vocal expression, "I need to see the priest, now."

My prayers were finally answered as a man in a white gown approached us from the left, "What is going on out here?"

She pointed her extended, right, index finger in my direction, "She wanted to speak to you, but I informed her that you are busy and she is refusing to leave."

His vision danced over me, "Follow me."

I gave him a slight nod of gratitude, "Yes, father."

At first, the walk between us was silent.

He cleared his throat twice before the letters came to the surface, "What can I do for you—uh."

I filled in the missing piece, "Samantha."

He nodded once in understanding, "What can I do for you today, Samantha?"

I exhaled deeply, not being sure where to start, "My house is haunted and I do not know what to do."

His eyes did not waiver from the pews ahead, "Why do you think this?"

I could feel the growl in my words, "I do not think anything, father. I know, there is something wrong with the house. I have been scratched and things disappear without reason. The lights and energy in the house get drained overnight. The vehicles will not start in the yard, we have to push them to the road. Things fly off of the walls, voices torment us at night when we are trying to sleep and that is just one-fourth of what I have been through."

The glossy coat to his green eyes stared down upon me, "Has it always been this bad or did something happen to provoke it?"

I found his question to be strange, the calmness of his tone surprised me.

My throat tightened as the answer grew in my chest, "No."

Before he had a chance to respond, I changed my answer, "Yes. I don't know. Maybe."

His tone remained strict, "I need to know what you are dealing with. Let me ask you something, Samantha. When was the last time you were in confession?"

An irritated sigh left the back of my throat, "I do not remember."

The dryness of his tone brushed against me, "When was the last time you went to church?"

I could feel irritation bubbling inside, "Can you come to the house and bless it?"

His lips tightened sharply, "I am afraid I cannot. I am sorry for the disappointment I have caused you, but I would never step a foot near that house. It is a miracle of God, himself that I am able to stand being around you."

CHAPTER SEVENTEEN:

HAUNTED

With no help being given from the priest, I headed out into the parking lot, towards the dark blue coupe that needed major work done. I pushed a deep sigh from my parted lips as I lowered my body into the drivers side compartment.

It took me a while to even turn the car over. I could not tell which bothered me more, his fear or my ability to live there.

A slight headache began to line my temples, along with the pain, an idea started brewing inside of my brain waves, *'Maybe, I would feel better if I could somehow understand what is happening.'*

A few moments later a shot of negativity tried to overtake my mind, *'Where the hell am I going to go to find out anything about this?'*

I pondered my options, when one stood out against the others, *'Go to a library.'*

My mood suddenly shifted with a dosage of hope. I put the vehicle into drive and started to travel towards the heart of the small town.

It took me less than ten minutes to get to the destination. While I was there, I went through book after book then I switched to the internet. After four hours of doing research, I found only one thing that made even the slightest bit of sense as to why this was happening.

It turned out that the *trail of tears* was directly walked on my property.

My mind started to intake the information, when a dark feeling overcame my form, *'Was it the Indians, who died on the trail of tears? Where they upset that we built a house on their land? Was something darker residing inside of the house? If so, how did it get there? It is true that I am attracting them due to the sixth sense. Was it my Father's death inside of the house? Was it the Ouija board? Or, a combination of everything happening in the same area?'*

I could not tell which option I wanted to look further into first.

My biggest fear was that it was all of the above reasons mixing together. The more information I found, the stronger the feeling to run overtook my figure.

It turned out that a lot of the Native Americans died on or around our land, but did they know they have passed on and need to go towards the light to get to the other side? Were they thinking we were the people who hurt them? Were they trying to get revenge?

I released a deep breath, not wanting to leave the library, but I knew I had a lot to do at the house and time was against me.

I got home thirty minutes later. I decide I just wanted to sit in the driveway. The dark energy was so powerful I wanted to put a bullet in my head.

All I could do was try my best to battle the feelings in my brain structure.

I could not help but to wonder, *'Was I too late?'*

With the little information I was able to find on the property itself, I wanted to know more. Almost like an addict, craving to get a better fix.

The research was hit hard on paranormal investigations, spirits, angels and the truth of what happened when we pass onto the next world. The information brought me a sense of peace and fear all in one, but I did not let it stop me from trying to do investigations myself. If nobody else was going to help me, I had to do it alone.

CHAPTER EIGHTEEN:

NO ESCAPE

I had read that doing remodeling on a home can have a huge impact on the afterlife. Depending on how strong the attachment to the house or property was when they were alive, but this did not fit, either. We put the house on the land and nobody else ever lived in it.

The more I packed, the worse it became. Almost as if they were angry about our departure.

It had become so intense and strong, the haunting started to follow me everywhere I would go. I could feel the energy around me being so down and depressive, something I never had happen to me before. It was almost like living in a constant abusive relationship with no light at the end of the tunnel.

Things in my car would go missing. When I would look into my rear-view mirror, I would see something dark and hazy in the back seat.

I felt completely trapped, when I would stay at other people's houses. Strange things would start affecting them as well. Of course, when their keys would go missing, the electronics would die or act up in my presence, they did not think it was anything more than just a strange day. Things would randomly fall or break without a logical reason for why it was happening, but I felt guilty, never being able to explain to them why.

After it got worse, I felt more afraid than ever before and it finally started to make sense. I am the one who is somehow channeling these actions to occur. The saddest part was, it did not just affect me.

CHAPTER NINETEEN:

THE SURGERY

Seven days had passed since my Mother was rushed to the hospital for her heart problems. Today was the day she was set to have the surgery done.

The operation was set to take seven to eight hours to complete. There was a sixty percent chance that she was not going to make it through the operation.

While she was out, I spent three hours in the chapel, praying for her to make it through this hard time and to prosper and live a very long, healthy, happy life.

The remaining time, I went home and tried to finish up the packing. I needed something to distract my mind from what was happening with my Mother.

With the majority of the house already packed up, I started to load the jeep with boxes. I drove thirty minutes to the new place of residency.

I was only able to do one load before an incoming call from a random mess of jumbled numbers that I did not recognize came through on the screen.

I answered with a broken tone, "Hello?"

The woman on the other line spoke quickly,

"Hello, Samantha?"

I was barely able to get my answer out, "Yes?"

She did not waste any time, transferring the information, "Hi there. I am calling you on behalf of your Mother from the hospital. She just got out of surgery, everything is going to be okay. The operation went well."

She hung up the phone before I could respond.

My emotions were so overpowering, I had to pull over on the side of the road, breaking down into a mess of tears, "Thank you, God. Thank you. I was so afraid that I was going to lose her. Thank you."

When I finally had my blurred vision under control. I once again headed straight for the hospital. I parked with no care about the situation of the vehicle.

I jumped out of the coupe, grabbing the cross off of the front, passenger seat.

I ran towards the building with a long stride.

I rushed in a state of urgency towards the elevator, reading the blue backgrounds with white letters of a directory. It stated that *ICU* was on the third floor.

It felt like it took forever to get into the right place. I nearly tripped over my own feet as I stumbled towards the nurse's station.

I spoke in a rapid fire of speech, "Can you tell me what room, Teresa Gollakner is in?"

The woman did not seem surprised to see me, "Yes, I will take you back there right now."

I followed the swishing notice of her white scrubs leading me down a maze of doors.

She slowed her stride to walk next to me, speaking in a state of concern, "I do have to warn you. She looks like someone had beaten her up. It is just from the surgery. She is okay and should still be sleeping when we enter. You cannot stay long, she needs her rest. Having you in there could cause her to come out of sedation sooner than what we would like her to."

My voice seemed to have been lost as I nodded my head in approval.

She used her right, index finger to point towards an open door to our right.

The moment I stepped over the threshold, I looked around for her. She was swollen on every inch of her body. The colors of yellow, swirling with blue and purple lined her face as tubes came out of her chest and stomach to release the fluid buildup in her lungs and chest cavity.

My whole body collapsed into the nurse. Seeing the woman, I have always known to be so strong, to being like this was too much for me to bear.

The nurse saw all of the color drain from my face. She automatically rushed me out of the room, into the hallway.

Her form flooded with concern, "Are you okay?"

The weight of my head fell forward in response, "That was just really hard to see her like that."

She nodded her head once in understanding, "Here, I will take that cross from you. Why don't you go home and get some sleep for a while? I will call you when she wakes up."

Once I got the call, I rushed into the room to see her.

She greeted me with a groggy discomfort, "I am so tired."

My voice shook, "Are you okay?"

She did not respond to the comment, instead she created a different conversation, "Did you finish packing, yet?"

My response was weak, "No."

She squinted her closed eyes as if in pain, "Go do that. I will call you later. Right now, I just want to sleep, okay?"

I nodded once before departing the room to her request.

CHAPTER TWENTY:

THE ATTACK

I had called a friend, who lived a few streets behind me, her voice sounded groggy on the other end of the line, "Hello?"

My tone cracked as it left my throat, "What are you doing?"

A small yawn slipped out, "Me and Rex are still sleeping. Is everything okay?"

I quickly pulled the phone away from my face to check the time, it was seven at night.

I nodded my head slightly, picturing the messy strands of her dark hair and closed green eyes as she laid with the tired figure of her husband. Who was sprawled out along his side of the bed, lacking structure to his black hair and fluttering, hazel vision.

The silence growing between us, brought my mind back to reality, "I need help moving. Can you guys help me with the bigger stuff? If not, that is okay, I understand."

Her high-pitched reply stung the inside of my left ear, "We would love to help. We will start getting dressed, see you soon."

My body decompressed, hearing that I will not have to be in the house alone for long, "Thank you so much. You have no idea how much this means to me."

I can hear the rustling of her pulling her figure out of the hold of the sheets, "Anytime, honey."

They arrived at the dwelling faster than I expected.

Rex walked towards me in a confident stride, "So, let me get this straight. You are afraid of your house and that is why we are here?"

My vision shot towards the ground, seeing a glimpse of his light, brown work boots that were illuminated by the porch light, "Yes and no. I need help with some of the heavy furniture."

His silence informed me that he did not buy my story.

A deep breath was released from the chamber of my lungs, "Okay, fine. I am terrified of this house, alright?"

A loud chuckle entered the air, bouncing back off of the near houses and into my mind for a second time, "You guys are so funny. The wife, brought a camera with her, thinking that she will actually be able to catch something on video. Come on, let's go inside. There is nothing to be afraid of."

I swallowed roughly allowing him to lead the way.

The moment he stepped over the threshold, his words shot through the nearly empty house, "Hello, spirits living in this home. If you are real then do something to me. Scratch me, bite me, push me over—anything. Come on, you piece of shit, do something!"

A push of fear ran through my mind, thinking back to Michael, "Maybe, you should not do that, Rex. You have no idea how they will react to you."

He threw his arms into the air, in a vulnerable stance leaving his body unprotected, "See, nothing is here. It is all in your head."

He followed me into one of the bedrooms to take apart the wooden frame of an old waterbed.

I could see the glisten of sweat running down his face.

He turned his head towards me, wiping the drops from his head onto the back of his forearm, "Is it not hot in here to you?"

I shook my head slowly, "No. It is kind of cold, actually."

He did not think too much about it, throwing his mind back towards unscrewing the bed set.

Roughly three minutes later, he dropped the screwdriver, placing his right hand over his chest.

His face contoured into a painful expression as he stood trying to take large gulps of air, but his lungs seemed to be rejecting them.

I called out to his wife, "Come here, now!"

She rushed around the corner, "Is everything—"

Her concern turned into agony as she saw his current state, "Come on, Rex. We need to get you out of the house."

He did not argue, he stumbled towards the front door. We followed him closely, we had to make sure he was safe before we could do anything else. Once free from the confines, he leaned his body against the freshly stained, wooden railing.

His wife approached him from behind, she placed her right hand on his back in a gentle caress, "Do I need to call 9-1-1, for you?"

The weight of is head pushed into a small shake, "No. I am fine. I am starting to feel better already. I do not know what came over me, all I know is that it is starting to subside."

His vision fell on me, "Okay. I believe you. Something is wrong with that house."

His wife patted him three times in a comforting manner, "We are going to go inside and take more pictures, I was able to get a few before you got sick. I caught some orbs, do you want to go in there again?"

He shook his head sharply, "No, you go ahead. I am going to stay out here and enjoy the beautiful weather."

Her face shifted from wonder to concern, "Are you sure you do not want to go in? Would it make you feel any better if I just took you home then came back here?"

He shook his head attempting to catch his breath, "As long as I do not have to go back in there, I will be just fine."

Her voice flooded with excitement, with us now being in the house of dim lighting and powerful energy, "Okay. You go stand over there in the center of the living room and I will take your picture."

I wandered over to where she was pointing with her right, index finger only moments prior, "Right here?"

With the camera aimed towards me, she nodded once in approval.

The flash burned my eyes as they attempted to readjust. She stared at the camera with a confused concerned plastered along the structure of her face.

A shot of fear ran through my stomach as I questioned, "What is wrong?"

She swallowed hard, "Nothing. Come over here. I want to take a picture of the empty room."

I was walking towards her, when the flash blasted the space with a brief light.

My curious mind pulled me towards the final outcome. I leaned over, seeing that no signs of ghosts are anywhere to be seen.

She completely ignored my attempt to relieve the tension that was hanging heavily in the air.

Her mind was only set on one thing, "Go stand in the kitchen."

I silently followed her demands, she rose the camera towards her face, "I changed my mind, lay on the floor where your dad died."

I did as she said, "Like this?"

My eyes were then blinded momentarily, she looked down at the picture.

I began walking towards her to investigate further before I have a chance, she barked an order, "Let's go into the back yard."

I lead her out the exit, onto the large patio.

She pointed her right, index finger towards the grassy area of the acre lot, "Go stand out there, I will take your photo."

I released a muffed, "Okay."

She snapped the image, she took a small look over the final image, this caused her voice to shake, "I think I know what is going on here. The house is not what is haunted, you are."

My eyes squinted in a hidden concern, "What do you mean?"

She stumbled over her words, the steadiness of her hands trembled, showing me the photos, "Every picture that does not have you in it—look, no orbs. Every time I snap one of you, there are at least five to six orbs that seem to be attached to you."

I swallowed roughly, "I was born three months early. Do you think it had something to do with that?"

Her shoulders moved slightly, "I have no idea, but it is getting late. Me and Rex both have to work tomorrow."

I nodded my head once in understanding.

All of the sudden, we were able to hear the call of Rex, "Get over here now!"

We rushed through the house and out the front door.

She took in a broken breath, "What is it? What is wrong?"

Half of his body was in the drivers seat, with his left leg dangling out of the white SUV, "The vehicle will not start."

My mind clicked with the answer, "Oh, yeah! Right, I completely forgot about this. We have to push it to the road. It has something to do with the haunting."

He sighed deeply, "This is just crazy. Why don't you come to stay with us tonight?"

I shook my head gently, "I can't. I have things that I need to get done. Anyway, I sleep in the car, but as I recently found out, it does not matter where I go, it follows me. Thank you for trying to give me a way out of this mess, that really means a lot to me."

CHAPTER TWENTY-ONE:

THE SEARCH

Just because I got out of the house, does not mean that the nights were quiet. It had been five years since I lived in the house of terrors. Yet, I still found pieces of the paranormal world everywhere I looked.

I remember when I thought it was actually going to stop when I left, but this time it was different.

Thankfully, the house was bright, I could no longer feel the violent heaviness that choked me when I walked into the door of the old house.

I still could hear voices in the hallway, nothing more than a quiet whisper calling out to me. They are always male voices, something about that spirit makes me think that he might have followed me to the new house and will continue to follow me for the rest of my life.

He has never done anything other than saying a few words. A few months after moving in, a dark laughter flooded the house from a side bathroom, but maybe, that was just my mind picking up on a higher vibration than I normally had on the days I could understand him.

The floors that ran down the hallway and into the

kitchen, creaked and moaned under your weight. In the middle of the night, I could still hear the sound of someone pacing the area.

The constant feeling of someone or something watching me, was still one of the worst things I had to battle or overcome, yet within myself. Or, maybe it was someone who thought I could help them and was trying to tell me who they are or where they are, that they were in distress.

I still found that my things would go missing and I would either never see them again or they would be put in a place that I would have never put them in.

There had been many incidents that happened in the new house that caused my body to jolt. The sound of someone smacking their lips at night, like they just ate a delicious meal or the scratching of nails running down the wall beside where I laid my head at night but still, there I was five years later about to move into a new place yet again and I still had no real answers.

I think it was about time I took my life back. This move was going to be different, I was finally going to break free—I had to. This darkness had hung over me for far too long. Someone—somewhere, had to be able to give me answers to that madness.

CHAPTER TWENTY-TWO:

THE FOLLOW

This time moving, I decided to try something different. Throughout all of my research over the years I had found that sometimes things can be attached to items.

So, as I was looking around the area, I realized that there were many things around me that I saw from the first house. The feeling in itself made me uneasy as I looked at each one trying to figure out what I need to get rid of.

Finally, after days of thinking about which items give me the worst feeling, I decided to just get rid of everything in the house, new or old and completely start over.

That sounded like a sure way to make whatever this was go away forever this time, right? Well, over the course of the next few weeks I watched anxiously as strangers came in and out of the house picking different items.

Part of me was holding my breath every time someone would walk in, not knowing if just the presence of the darkness lurking in the shadows would be enough to push them out the door. No one seemed to pick up on anything negative, they were all very nice people. Each item walking out the door gave me a sense of relaxation and guilt.

I could not help but pray that the articles leaving were finally the ones to set me free. Yet, I found myself feeling horrible that one of these nice people are going to end up getting the darkness themselves.

I tried to alleviate my mind, '*It was only after me, right? You saw that it talked to you on the Ouija board, you know that its main mission was to come here to destroy you. It will not hurt someone else, just you.*'

My pep talks seemed to help me sleep at night, but every single time I would go back into the house to finish packing, the air still felt stale. Boxes were still rattling and noises bounced through the halls with no explanation.

Finally, the day to start moving the bigger stuff arrived. There was one thing that I knew had to come with me, a statue of Mary outside of my house that belonged to my Mother. She always told me to keep her outside to protect me from all of the evil in the world. I felt at peace knowing that she was going to the new house, but it did make being in the old one harder to handle.

It made me feel naked and bare to the demons around me.

Later that day, a nice couple drove in from a town roughly forty minutes away to pick up an old dresser that used to belong to my Father's best friend when he was younger. The man died suddenly, my Dad wanted to keep the dresser in a remembrance of his friend.

I never knew this story until during the move. My Mother informed me of the details after hearing about me wanting to give it away. This seemed like it could actually be the answer that I was looking for. Maybe, once this dresser leaves, it would all be over.

The thought in itself made me giddy, I wanted to get it as far away from me and my house as possible. When they arrived, they began to look over the item.

I released a long, slow breath hearing her say that it was everything that they were looking for and she was going to use it for one of her daughters.

I replied in a fake fit of laughter, not knowing what to say or if I should say anything at all.

I decided it was best just to let nature take its course and have faith in the fact that whatever it was only wanted to harm me.

Seeing it leave the front door, I made my way to the patio to have a cigarette. Each drag of smoke counted another second that passed since it left my hands and into theirs.

The smile on my face quickly faded seeing that a black shadow was heading from their car towards my house.

I gasped slightly, nearly choking on my cigarette as it disappeared into the slab of concrete beneath my feet.

A harsh swallow formed inside of my throat as I wandered back into the house. The air has once again shifted to a heavy despair, shattering my hopes and reconstructing the nightmare.

The weight of my head shook in a slow motion, *'Whatever this is, still has to be attached to something in the house. I just have to keep searching until I find it.'*

Finally, everything was gone. Looking around at the empty dwelling made me want to both laugh and cry.

Laugh for the fact that this situation is going to finally come to an end. Maybe, some real answers will come of all the madness. Then I wanted to cry for looking around at the nothingness that I now have to rebuild due to fear.

The fear of something so cowardly that it has to be invisible during this battle.

A few days later, I was doing some last-minute cleaning sweeps through the house when I heard my Mom calling me from the other room, "Come here, hurry!"

I took off down towards the room where I heard her voice coming from, panic flooded my tone, "What is it? What is wrong?"

Her shaken, right hand pointed towards the bathroom door between us and the contents, "The light is on, but I have not been in there. Have you?"

I shook my head slowly, "No. I will just turn it off.

Probably just forgot to turn it off one of the other days."

My open, right palm reached towards the golden handle, when I found that it was locked.

My eyebrows squished tightly together, *'I never lock this door, ever. This is really weird.'*

I turned towards my Mom, shrugging my shoulders gently, "I don't know what happened. It won't open."

Her face drained slightly in color, "Maybe, someone is in there. You had the front door open all day while you were moving things in and out. Maybe, someone got in."

She stepped towards the door, speaking in a deeper vibration, "Come on, open the door."

My right eye twitched slightly under the sound of her voice, "No one is in there. It probably just got locked on accident. I will go get my tools to get the door handle off."

She nodded once to me as I disappeared into the other room and then back in front of the door in a flash.

Once all of the parts were off of the door, I tried to pull the doorknobs apart, when it felt like someone was holding it in place on the other side.

A slight gasp fell from my lips, "Someone has to be in there. There is no reason that this door is not opening."

I dropped down towards the floor in a push-up position, taking a small peek under the door panel to see if I could get a glimpse of who was doing that, but nothing was there.

I quickly forced myself back onto my feet, "This is really weird and makes no sense. Something has to be in there. The doorknob should have come off already."

I refrained from speaking to turn all of my attention back onto the door. I used everything inside of me to try and pry the metal pieces apart. Finally, the entire door let free, throwing me into a backwards step to reveal that in fact, nobody was there.

It was the craziest feeling in the entire world, like someone had just ripped all the air out of the atmosphere and there was nothing left in that moment other than me and the emptiness of the room mocking me.

There I sat, everything gone and yet it was still there.

I became angry, hearing the imaginary laughter being released from its throat surrounding me as I thought to myself, '*I have to do something else.*'

My mind began to race back to all of my research, I ran out to the nearest natural store I could find and grabbed up a bundle of the white sage. Which from all of my scanning on the internet I found that sage can help cleanse a room and rid the home of bad energy. It was worth a shot, right?

I immediately got home to begin the process, but the minute I went through very room and felt no different, I soon realized that it was just another hope that would be shattered around me.

In that moment I could not help but to think, '*Is there ever going to be an end?*'

CHAPTER TWENTY-THREE:

THE HEALER

Over the course of the next few weeks in the new house, I realized that I was not feeling the best, physically, emotionally or mentally. I went to the doctor, but they were never able to figure out what was going on with me. They would do tests after tests, but no answer could ever be found. It always haunted me a bit, leaving the doctor's office to find that I was in no better shape than when I walked in. I went home and decided to listen back to the last taped session I had with my Medium, Brenda.

She told me that I had a strong energy around me, something powerful and that I needed to go to an energy healer in hopes of having it released.

I had listened to this recording many times before, always looking for a different answer of course, but this was the first time this statement really stood out to me, *'What if, the house was never haunted? What if, nothing was attached to the things I had? What if, it was attached to me this entire time?'*

I immediately ran towards my phone, looking for

the best energy healer in the DFW area. Finally, I found one that I felt good about her name was Debra and she was able to get me in ASAP when I spoke to her on the phone, she could tell it was urgent.

Ever since I could remember I had suffered from severe anxiety. It was getting to the point that I would pace the house for hours on end, looking for some kind of answer to the questions that burried themselves into my mind at night. I imagine that she could sense this about me through the phone.

On my way there, I felt like I was going to lose my mind. The GPS started acting crazy. It shut down my phone, forcing me to completely miss my exit and have to turn around, making me go about twenty minutes out of my way.

I felt more frustrated than ever on my way there. I could feel the anger and energies bubbling up inside of me, yet they had nowhere to go, but out of my mouth into the stale air surrounding me.

Part of me could not help but to wonder, '*Was this creature, this being, getting pleasure and enjoyment out of watching me suffer?*'

I pulled up to the line of businesses in this small strip mall just outside of the major city of Fort Worth.

I took a deep inhale of air, before pulling myself out of the car, four minutes before our appointment.

It took almost everything inside of me to make it to the door.

The vibrations of my clinched, right fist pounded against the wooden barrier between us.

To my surprise, nobody came to the door. I tried to knock one more time.

Finally, I could hear footsteps moving around inside.

The clash of the dead bolt breaking free from the panel rang through my mind as the door swung in an inwards movement towards an elderly woman in a dark blue dress with short gray hair staring at me with a smile, "Please, come on in. I am sorry that it took me a minute to get to the door. I was in the bathroom when I heard you knock the first time. Figures."

I greeted her back with a small grin, "It is okay."

She nodded her head twice in confirmation that we are in fact on the same page, "Come on over here, Cynthia."

I could not help but to laugh, capturing her attention, "Is something wrong?"

Through a mouthful of laughter, I explained briefly, "My name is Samantha, not Cynthia."

She threw her head back firmly, "Oh yes, right. I

am sorry about that, Samantha. I have another new client, her name is Cynthia. Sorry about that mess up."

My demeanor appeared to have relaxed a few notches. I followed her into a back room, where she had a nice set up with a massage bed and a pillow laying in the middle by the legs.

A nice sound box to the left, that released streams of music into the air, creating a peaceful realm of contentment to surround me.

She motioned towards the bed, "Lay down on your stomach or your back, it does not matter. Whichever side you want to start with. It is completely up to you. This is your hour session, you have to make the most out of it for yourself."

I smiled up at her gently, "Thank you, ma'am."

I proceed to get onto the bed, laying with my face towards the ceiling.

Debra walked up behind me, placing a washcloth over my eyes to allow me to remain focused during the session.

I nodded my head once, taking a deep breath trying to relax my body as much as possible.

Finally, I begin to doze off into the atmosphere, part of my hearing was tuned into Debra, walking silently around me doing what she had to, ensuring that my energy was being cleansed. The other part of my brain was lost in hopes and dreams about how amazing my life was going to be after this is all removed.

Suddenly, I felt her pulling against my feet as she called out to me, "Samantha. Okay, I want you to start slowly bringing yourself back to reality. The session is over, you did really good. Start moving your hands and your toes to be able to ground yourself back to this room."

She aided me into a seated position, with my feet dangling off of the edge of the bed, "Well, I found something. There was a man, who I pulled out of your aura. In fact, your aura was so bad that it looked like a curtain and someone with really long nails decided to run their fingers down through it. I made him go away, I forced him into the light. I kept trying to ask him his name, but he would not give it to me. He finally gave me this small, evil grin then—poof. He vanished into the light. He is never going to be able to hurt you, again. It was black magic, someone put a hex on you. Who do you know that would do something like this?"

My mind began to scan every person that I had made contact with through my life, yet through all of the faces, I couldn't find one person that would match this kind of behavior.

I shrugged my shoulders gently, "I have no idea. I just really am glad that it is gone. Thank you so much.

So, now after this everything will be okay, right? And, I will feel better, too?"

She gave me the best smile she could conjure up, "Well, he has been around you for a very long time. And, he has caused many disturbances. Just now, in our reading do you know how the music kept stopping? That was him, he wanted to mess up your session. On your way here, when the GPS started to act up, that was him, too. He wanted to make sure that you never got here. He did not want to leave you and he knew that I would be able to see him and he did not like that. The first session, most people do not see results. Every two weeks, I want to see you. You released a lot of stuff today, but there is still a lot left inside of you, I can feel it. We need to work on this."

I nodded my head once in understanding, "Okay. Let's make the next appointment."

I believed everything she told me because I had not told her anything about myself.

Years ago, a medium told me a dark figure was trying to break into my aura and I never did tell her about the trouble with the GPS on the way there.

CHAPTER TWENTY-FOUR:

THE MEDIUM

As much as I wanted to just let this go and say that all things were meant to be, I couldn't.

The nights became harder and I became more afraid, of what? Whoever decided to put a curse on me.

I could not help but to wonder, *'If this person already had enough guts to curse me once, won't they find out that I am now no longer cursed and try and do it again?'*

The heaviness of this question left more pain than it did heal. I decided to seek out the help of my medium Brenda, again. I knew that she would be able to get a better reading on me because he was gone and no longer blocking her.

It felt like I was never going to be able to find peace in all of that chaos and she was my last hope.

Finally, I got the date and time set up for our appointment and the day I have been waiting for is finally beginning. Ever since we decided on a date, all I could think about was the reading.

I sat there and wondered all the questions that my brain could create, '*I wonder what she is going to tell me about this man? I cannot help but to wonder, who was he? What did he want and most importantly, who sent him? I wanted to ask her about my life and see where I need to improve on to be the best version of myself. What I need to do to get everything good that I want out of this life. She has never disappointed or read me wrong before, but I was nervous. Nervous of the answers that she was going to give me. What if they were not that answers that I had hoped for? Will they be enough to finally give me closure or will I be sitting here in a week trying to map out my next move?*'

The tension on the day of the call was unbearable. With her being back home in Milwaukee and me in Texas we could only do readings over the phone. She said that she was going to call me at four.

Phew, I had never known that time goes by so slowly until I had been waiting my whole life for a moment.

Finally, after an hour and a half past time, my phone began to ring, she answered with a groggy voice, "Hello, I am sorry that it took me so long to call. I had an emergency come up and I really needed to handle the call. I thought that I would have had this better planned out. Excuse me, sometimes things just slip my mind. So, I am sitting here and I am remembering that you sent me a picture of a house, what is that about?"

A slight laugh fell out of my throat and into the

air, "Yes. The house in the picture, that is my old house. I was wondering if you could tell me if it is haunted or not."

Her reply was fast, sending a chill to trail down my spine, "Yes. I only had to look at the picture once to have it in my head and the first moment I looked at it I could tell you yes, that is a very haunted area. Why? What is going on, are you feeling some kind of weird energy?"

I nodded my head in agreement as if it slipped my mind that she cannot see me, "Yes, well no. Actually, I do not live there anymore, but I followed your advice. The last time we talked, you told me to go to an energy healer. She told me that she pulled a man out of my aura and that someone had put a curse on me with black magic, she informed me that his main mission was to destroy my life."

A brief moment of laughter slipped out of her mouth, "I do not think that he was trying to ruin your life, exactly. He did not agree with a lot of things that you believe in or are doing and he would try to stop them from happening based off his own personal beliefs. I do not think that he would try to hurt you. Trust me, your dad would not let that happen. He was Native American. You did pick him up when you lived in that old house, that is when he attached himself to you. He has been there for a very long time. I am seeing that he did a lot of voodoo, but nobody sent him to you out of a curse. Sometimes, energy healers, are not very good at determining what kind of energy that are actually dealing with. She was absolutely right to get rid of him and send him into the light, but she was not sure why he was there. Does that make sense?"

I smiled gently, "Yes. That makes sense. What else can you tell me about him or that house?"

She exhaled sharply, "There is not much else that I am able to see other than the things that I already told you. Just have faith in God, keep your energy high and your thoughts clean and pure. Do not allow anything bad to ever come into your life again. He is gone now and you are never going to have to worry about him coming back."

I could feel the weight of my body fall into a relaxed placement, '*I cannot believe that this is finally over. I cannot believe that one man could cause so much pain, so much heart ache. I feel free. I do not know what I am going to do now that I do not have him there. I guess, I could do anything, right?*'

The thought in itself was enough to drift me off to sleep that night.

Roughly at three in the morning I felt like I could not breath. The upper portion of my body flew up into a seated placement. I grabbed the front of my throat with my open, right palm, gasping for each breath.

This time, it was only a nightmare.